HOW TO CATCH THE TOOTH FAIRY

WRITTEN BY
ADAM WALLACE

ILLUSTRATED BY
ANDY ELKERTON

Copyright © 2016 by Sourcebooks, Inc.
Cover design by Sourcebooks, Inc.
Written by Adam Wallace
Cover and internal illustrations © Andy Elkerton

Sourcebooks and the colophon are registered trademarks of Sourcebooks, Inc.

The art was first sketched, then painted digitally with brushes designed by the artist.

Published by Sourcebooks Jabberwocky, an imprint of Sourcebooks, Inc.
P.O. Box 4410, Naperville, Illinois 60567-4410
(630) 961-3900
Fax: (630) 961-2168
www.sourcebooks.com

The Library of Congress Cataloging-in-Publication data is on file with the publisher.

Source of Production: Leo Paper, Heshan City, Guangdong Province, China
Date of Production: May 2016
Run Number: 5005931

Printed and bound in China.
LEO 10 9 8 7 6 5 4 3 2 1

HOW TO CATCH THE TOOTH FAIRY

WRITTEN BY
ADAM WALLACE

ILLUSTRATED BY
ANDY ELKERTON

sourcebooks
jabberwocky

All is quiet, all is still.

The clock shows 3:09.

The bell goes off! I'll go to work,

'cause now's my time to **shine**!

I'm the **Tooth Fairy**, yes I am!
And every single night,
I collect three hundred thousand teeth
while staying out of sight!

My travels take me far and wide.

My life is such a **BLAST**!

But please don't try to catch me,

for I'm really much too fast!

At Nancy Caton's, I recall
an important fairy rule.
When you are taking someone's tooth,
watch out for all their drool!

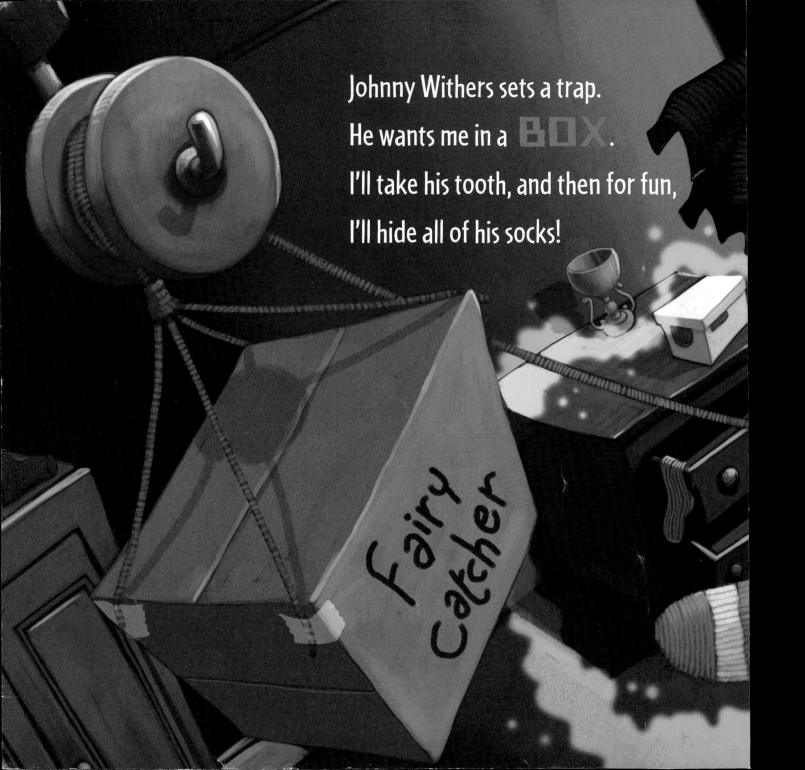

Johnny Withers sets a trap.

He wants me in a **BOX**.

I'll take his tooth, and then for fun,

I'll hide all of his socks!

Fairy Catcher

Cotton candy? Love the stuff!
But I won't try to eat it.
Every trap that's set for me
is sure to be defeated!

Julie has a good idea:
a trap made out of *floss*!
I'll get her tooth, then leave a coin
to pay her for her loss.

As I fly to Taylor's bed,

I notice something scary.

But once I've tied it all in knots,

I'm feeling rather merry!

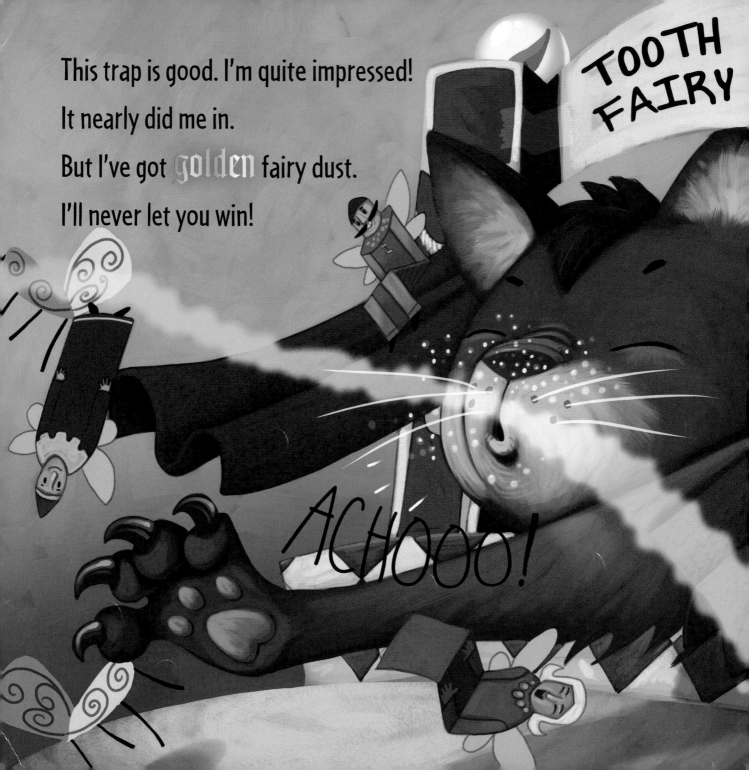

The lights are off in Sarah's room,
and traps are everywhere!
I'll need to do my *fairy best*
to fly safe out of there!

Now Sanjeev is creative.

He's made a SPECIAL CAGE.

Am I no more? Is this the end?

You'd better turn the page...

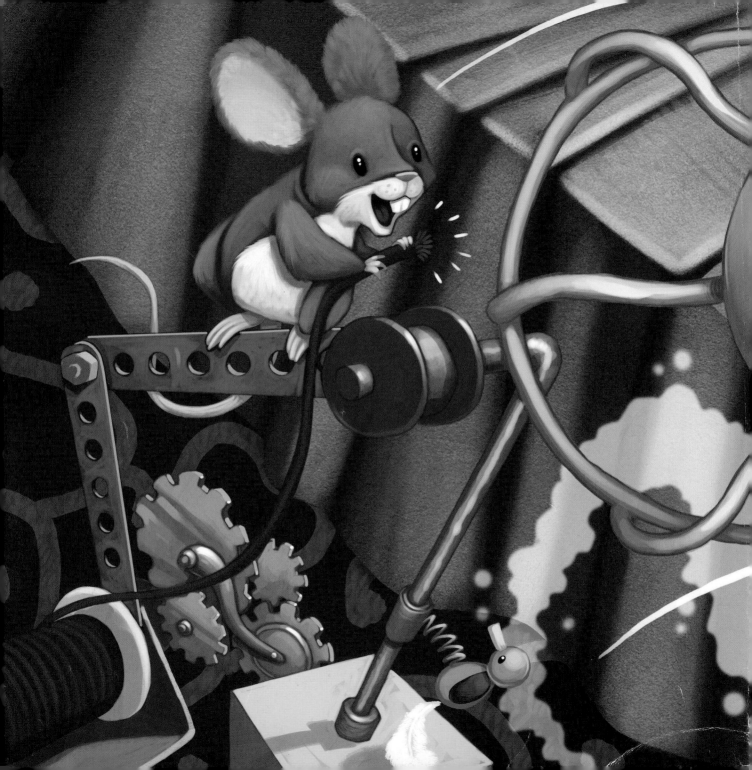

And then, at last, I'm home again.

The teeth are safe and sound.

The kid who'll catch me in a trap

is still yet to be found.